The Fight For My Daughter

by Howard Zoldessy

Copyright © 2025 Howard Zoldessy.

Disclaimer: This work is a fictitious creation. Names, characters, places, and incidents are the product of the author's imagination. Any resemblance to actual persons living, dead, or on life support, or any business entities, events, venues, or settings is purely coincidental.

All rights reserved, including the right of reproduction in whole or in part in any form.

ORANGE TABBY PUBLISHING

Knoxville, Tennessee, USA

Cover Art and design by Maria Loysa-Bel Nueve – de los Angeles

Paperback ISBN: 978-1-963281-13-2, 978-1-963281-14-9
Hardback ISBN: 978-1-963281-15-6

Printed in the United States of America.

The Fight For My Daughter

Nothing could have prepared him for what was coming. He had protected his family against hardship and misfortune. He could not have planned for the inconceivable. There was no map for navigating these waters, no wisdom from an elder or advice from an astute colleague. There were only his instincts, ingenuity, and guile.

He learned to manage the agonizing abyss of waiting. In her final days, under the spell of morphine, his young and beautiful wife slept peacefully in the master bedroom. In the family room, their four-year-old daughter rested her head upon his right shoulder. Within a few minutes, she drifted off to sleep. He placed the well-worn copy of Goodnight Moon on the coffee table and carried Sadie to her bedroom. He tucked her in, turned on the monitoring device, and plugged in the nightlight.

Back in the family room, he opened the sliding glass door and stepped onto the screened patio. He gave ear to the emerging brood of cicadas, a synchronized, thunderous buzzing so powerful the echo created a rhythmic downbeat. Dormant and then irrepressible, he admired their behavior.

Hudson never had intended to become Sadie's primary parent. He had presumed his role would be similar to that of the millions of fathers who had come before him. He attended birthing classes, reworked the family budget, and researched college tuition programs. Although Marilyn's obstetrician said everything looked normal, a voice he could not silence told him otherwise. Marilyn's fatigue was beyond what Hudson had expected, and her baby bump was not as rotund as it should have been. Nudged by intuition, he purchased and devoured three instructional books for new parents.

Sadie arrived by express train, thirty days ahead of schedule. Within twenty-four hours of her birth, the Neonatal Intensive Care Unit handed Hudson a packet containing a catalogue of the challenges and obstacles his premature daughter would encounter during her lifetime. Hudson was told Sadie would lag behind in school and might have processing and social interaction issues. He folded and tucked the preemie literature into the inside breast pocket of his blazer. "I appreciate your concern," Hudson told the director of the newborn unit. "I will certainly read this material. The statistics, or whatever they are will not define Sadie. She will write her own story."

After three days in an incubator, Sadie was discharged from the NICU. The transfer of responsibility took place under the canopy at the hospital's main entrance. During the final handover, the nurse uttered a two-word sentence that Hudson shall never forget. "Enjoy her," the nurse said.

Marilyn had intended to breastfeed, but she could not produce milk. At four in the afternoon on Sadie's first day home, Hudson purchased baby formula, plastic bottles, and bottle liners.

Following his daughter's cues, he fed her every three hours. They sat on the rocking chair in Sadie's room as she suckled formula and snuggled against her dad's fleece sweatshirt. Having read that infants are most comfortable in mother's soft embrace, he had purchased a thick, merino wool fleece to cushion his lean, boney frame. He also enhanced Sadie's plush feeding and burping station with a tender, high-pitched voice. His books had taught him that infants also favor mother's soft register over father's deeper tones.

Although father and daughter occasionally fell asleep in the rocker, Sadie usually slept in her crib. Marilyn's irregular sleeping habits required Hudson to bunk on the couch in his home office near Sadie's bedroom. When Marilyn had the energy, she fed Sadie in the master bedroom while Hudson prepped meals, cleaned house, or processed laundry.

Publicly, he supported the consensus that Marilyn's lethargy was caused by postpartum hormonal fluctuations. Privately, he suspected something more serious.

Hudson hired a private nanny to help with Sadie and the household chores. During the week, Hudson waited for the nanny before he left for the office. She usually arrived by seven. Hudson drove home to check on his family at eleven and again at three. When he returned with groceries and supplies at six, the nanny would discreetly brief him about the interaction between Marilyn and her parents: "They always seem to know when you won't be around. There's usually a lot of hush-hush conversation going on."

Hudson's business obligations required him to regularly inspect a portfolio of commercial properties, including two outliers fifty miles north of Palm Beach County. Every second Wednesday, thirty minutes after Marilyn swallowed her sleeping aid and just after Sadie's nine o'clock feeding, Hudson's younger brother guarded the fort. Hudson completed his inspection and his one hundred mile round trip in time for Sadie's midnight bottle. Hudson managed the household, Marilyn's comfort, Sadie's care and well-being, and his business interests. Hudson adapted to four hours of sleep.

Marilyn and Hudson celebrated Sadie's first birthday with their extended family. The following day, Marilyn dropped the hammer: "Hudson, I want a divorce. I'm not happy. I feel neglected. You work too many hours. I'm lonely. I want more. Sadie and I are leaving."

Hudson was devastated. Marilyn explained that she was going to meet her former boyfriend in Orlando in two weeks: "He's divorced and has custody of his five-year-old son. I want Sadie to meet them." Marilyn revealed that her parents had arranged the Orlando meeting, and they would be financing the trip, the divorce, and her resettlement. "Sadie and I will live with my parents until I can move into my own place. They're already setting up our bedrooms."

Marilyn's words were polished steel that pierced Hudson's heart. Although she expressed empathy, Marilyn downplayed the bond between Sadie and her dad: "I have a right to be happy, Hudson. And you can see Sadie on holidays." Hudson had no words to describe his anger and his pain. He could not lose his daughter.

Hudson's initial reaction was to buy himself some time. He asked Marilyn to reconsider, explaining that a divorce would impact Sadie and break apart her family. "She's young enough to recover," Marilyn said. "She may not even remember you or that we were even married."

"Losing you as my wife hurts beyond description. But if that's what you want, if you want to take up with your old boyfriends, you have that right. But I cannot lose Sadie. I will do everything in my power not to lose my daughter." Hudson's intense expression transmitted anger. The furrowed lines in his brow and his dilated pupils punctuated his assertion. Hudson detected a slight recoil in Marilyn's posture as he added, "Before you make a definitive move, I'm asking you to reconsider."

In the morning, from the privacy of his office, Hudson sought legal guidance. A retired judge, for whom Hudson had brokered several profitable real estate investments, offered the name of a brilliant family law attorney. Preventing Sadie from traveling to Orlando for Marilyn's rendezvous was Hudson's first goal. Hudson knew his marriage was over. He saw it in Marilyn's eyes. And she saw something in Hudson's eyes, a fierce determination not to lose his daughter.

The magistrate's closing remark was deeply distressing: "It is painfully apparent to me that your wife's parents have the resources and connections to get what they want and send you into financial oblivion. You may have bought yourself a few days, but Marilyn's parents will insulate her and control the process, legally and otherwise."

Hudson concealed his torment from his colleagues and associates. Before leaving for home for his eleven o'clock check-in, he hustled into the photocopy room and checked his mail cubby. A flyer circulated by the Human Resources

Department caught his attention. His employer had a job opening in Knoxville, Tennessee. Hudson photocopied the flyer, secured the original and the duplicate into two separate binders, and left the office.

In the days following Marilyn's gut-wrenching announcement, Hudson and Marilyn continued to cohabitate. He managed to cloak his anguish. Despite the curtain of estrangement, Hudson maintained his normal domestic schedule, tending to both Marilyn and Sadie. No one was going to stop him from nurturing and supporting his daughter. He believed, with every fiber of his being, that only God could separate him from Sadie.

One week later, the nanny informed Hudson that Marilyn had complained about abdominal pain. That evening, after Hudson fed, bathed, and launched Sadie into dreamland, he and Marilyn researched the possible causes of her discomfort. Endometriosis seemed likely, so Hudson called Marilyn's OBGYN practice and left a message with the after-hours receptionist. A nurse returned the call and set a morning appointment. Marilyn's pain intensified overnight. At nine in the morning, her doctors performed a laparoscopic procedure to confirm endometriosis. Hudson waited alone in the surgical wing. Two hours passed before a female physician clad in a surgical gown asked him to step into a private office. Her expression was dour. "I'm sorry to be the one to tell you this. Your wife has ovarian cancer. The oncologist is classifying her as stage 4." Hudson nearly fell out of his chair. He managed to speak through his shock, disbelief, and horror. The surgeon explained that an invasive surgery and then several rounds of chemotherapy would follow. From that moment two thoughts dominated Hudson's existence: Prolonging Marilyn's life and protecting Sadie.

Three weeks after the diagnosis, Marilyn underwent a five-hour surgery. Hudson waited alone in the hospital. He asked every question on his notepad in the limited face time debriefing with the surgical oncologist. Hudson then called Marilyn's parents with an update and waited another hour before being allowed into recovery. Sadie spent the day with her nanny.

That evening, Hudson sensed that Sadie was aware of her mother's absence. After Sadie's bath, he drove her to the hospital parking lot and pointed out Marilyn's room. "Sadie, do you see that light up there? Mommy's in that room. She told me to tell you that she loves you, and she'll be home soon."

The day before Marilyn was released, Hudson met at home with a morphine nurse and then a colostomy nurse. The master bedroom was transformed into a hospital room. Two weeks after the surgery, Hudson sat with Marilyn in the infusion center. Twenty-four hours later, Marilyn's violent reaction to the chemotherapy exceeded the oncology team's description of what to expect. Marilyn needed three days to recover. Hudson had become the primary caregiver to his terminally ill wife as well as their one-year-old daughter.

Hudson refused to allow the unfolding tragedy to traumatize Sadie. After her diagnosis, Marilyn agreed with Hudson that Sadie should be sheltered from the misery. Hudson studied the parenting guides for raising children born prematurely. He created a nurturing plan for circumventing any development issues before they could manifest. As Sadie approached her second birthday, Hudson incorporated interactive museum exhibits, children's theater, zoos, and playgrounds into their father-daughter agenda. After dinner they played with toys designed to promote hand-eye coordination and games to encourage problem solving. Sadie gravitated toward jigsaw puzzles and ring toss. Hudson devised a three-step program for teaching Sadie how to read. They sang the lyrics to the songs on popular TV shows until Sadie memorized them. Then Hudson played the videos of those songs on the TV with the closed captioning activated. When he muted the volume, Sadie began to recognize words and could sing the songs on her own. Her word recognition vocabulary grew with the introduction of fresh videos. Sadie and her dad sang and read in the evenings after dinner and after breakfast on weekends. By her third birthday, Sadie was recognizing several dozen words by sight.

Over the span of three years, Marilyn endured nine additional rounds of chemotherapy followed by nine violent reactions. Hudson was at her side for every round of chemo and the sickening aftermath. He had never seen such suffering.

One week before Marilyn's second surgery, her parents stopped by. In the family room they quietly chatted with the morphine nurse: "She's comfortable," the nurse reported. "I told her she doesn't have to wear that wig for me. If you need me, I'll be here for another hour."

The bedroom smelled like the hospital cancer wing. Marilyn was resting in the center of the king-size bed, holding the TV remote in her right hand. In her left hand she held a handset with a large button. The handset was connected to a patient-controlled analgesic pump that dispensed morphine through an infusion port that was surgically attached to a vein on the left side of Marilyn's upper chest, just below her collarbone. A collection of medicine vials and supplement bottles were arranged by frequency of use on the right side table. A black wig rested on the left table, behind the colostomy supplies. The blinds were closed to block the bright Florida sunshine.

The patient mustered a smile. Marilyn's mother sat beside her and held her left hand. Her father placed a worn leather binder on the bed and stood beside her mother. "Where did he take her this time?" her father asked.

"They're at the children's museum. Sadie loves the kids' grocery store."

"I bet he'll show up five minutes after we leave," her father said as he reached for the binder. "Marilyn, we need to talk. This is a tough subject, but we have to address it, and we don't want anyone else to know." Marilyn's mother dried her eyes as her husband continued: "We pray for the best outcome, but we have to be prepared for the worst. If, God forbid, something happens to you, we need to raise Sadie. We can give her a great life. We can give her everything she'll ever need. He can't give her what she'll need, financially, emotionally, or in any other way. We don't want her living alone with him. God knows what he would do to her or where she'd end up. With us she'll be happy. With him she'll have a terrible life. Is that what you want? We think he'll be relieved for us to raise Sadie. I would even write him a check to give him a fresh start somewhere else. But if he wants to stick around, we'd let him see Sadie every so often under our supervision, but only if she wants to see him. Sadie will need a mother, and he's no mother. I don't even think he's a good father."

"Let's just focus on Sadie's welfare," Marilyn's mother said.

"Your mother's right," Marilyn's father said, and then he removed a document from the binder and handed it to his daughter.

"What's this?" Marilyn asked.

"It's a custody agreement. It says you want your daughter to be in our care and custody if something should happen to you."

"Have you discussed this with Hudson?" Marilyn asked.

"Not yet. We think he'll agree."

"Sadie loves her dad," Marilyn said.

"And Sadie could still see him, if that's what she wants. If he's not around, she'll just forget him. We've been dealt a horrible hand. Before you got sick, you told him you wanted a divorce. We were never enamored of him when you were dating, but we kept it to ourselves. We thought he was too old for you, and too conservative."

"Why didn't you say anything?"

"We didn't want to interfere with your happiness, so we looked the other way. And when his parents went broke and lost their home, we knew they were beneath us. That family is a bunch of frauds. He married you under false pretenses.

If you had filed for divorce, I would have gotten you custody, and that would have enhanced our position now. Maybe I haven't practiced for ten years, but I still know the law and how judges think. The best interests of the child always come first, and your mother and I are Sadie's best alternative as parents. Let's see what the psychologist says. I'm absolutely certain she'll support our position. Let's proceed as if you had filed for a divorce with custody."

"If you spring this on Hudson, he might get an attorney," Marilyn said.

"That schmuck doesn't know the first thing about the court system," her father snapped, "and he doesn't have the money to hire a decent attorney anyway."

"I'm tired. I don't want to read this now. I want to sleep. I have another surgery coming up. I need to rest." Marilyn's father folded the document in half, placed it into a paperback book, and slid the book into the bottom draw of the right side table. "Do you see that brown suede sack in the back of the drawer?" Marilyn asked.

"Yes," her father answered.

"My three-carat engagement ring, my Rolex, and my pearl necklace are in that sack. There are too many strangers coming into this house. Please hold them for me."

"Of course. Your mother can put them into her safe deposit box."

"Mom, if I'm not here, please give that sack to Sadie when she grows up." Her mother tearfully nodded.

Marilyn's parents kissed her goodbye, locked the front door of the four-bedroom house, and drove home. Thirty minutes later, Sadie jumped onto the master bed and told her mother about shopping for groceries in the museum and then riding the pony at the park. When Sadie ran off, Hudson asked Marilyn how she was feeling.

"Hudson, after you put Sadie to sleep, we need to talk."

At nine that evening, Hudson pulled a chair up to Marilyn's bed. "Before we talk about Sadie, I want to thank you for taking care of me. It hasn't been easy for either of us. You didn't have to, but you did, so thank you."

"I wish it hadn't come to this," Hudson said, "but we'll get through it."

Marilyn blotted her tear ducts with a tissue and said, "I want to talk to you about Sadie. If I'm not here, if I'm gone, my parents want to raise her."

"Please don't give up. You're here right now. You're living and breathing. Concentrate on that. Cancer takes part of your body but all of your mind. Keep fighting! Let's just keep taking it one day at a time . . . or one hour, or one minute. Maybe we need a miracle, but miracles do happen, and as long as you're alive, you're a candidate for a miracle."

"But what if I die? I think I'm going to die, and my parents . . ."

"Is that what you want?" Hudson interrupted. "Do you think if Sadie loses her mom, she should lose her dad?"

"You could still be part of her life. But my mother wants to be Sadie's mom, and they both want Sadie to live with them."

Marilyn pressed the button to activate the morphine pump. Hudson waited for the payload to take effect before responding: "A single devoted dad can be a mother. I've been Sadie's mom and dad for these last four years, for her entire life, and I'm capable of providing a home. I don't want you to be concerned about this. You need to think about getting well. I don't know that every dad can also be a mom, but I can. Maybe that's my purpose."

"Oh, spare me. You make me laugh. How dare you say that's your purpose? I want my parents involved. Maybe they should raise her if you're that stupid."

"Did they put you up to this?"

"What difference does it make?"

"Your parents are putting their interests above everything else."

"My father has always been controlling, but this isn't about them. They want you to take Sadie to a psychologist. They made an appointment. I want you to go. I need you to go. Hudson, do it for me," Marilyn pleaded as she pressed the morphine button again.

Hudson projected acquiescence. He had no intention of walking Sadie into a trap and no intention of debating the issue with his morphine-addled wife, so he followed the expedient path: "Okay. That appointment will be honored."

"Oh, by the way, I gave my jewelry to my mother to hold for Sadie."

"Okay. But when you're in remission and cancer-free, your jewelry should be back in this house or in our safe deposit box."

Thirty minutes before the appointment with the psychologist, Hudson surveyed the parking lot. He did not recognize any of the cars. He then drove to the neighboring lots and spotted his father-in-law's gold Mercedes sedan parked next to a dumpster in the back of a strip center.

The psychologist greeted Hudson in the reception area. He measured her up. She was in her mid-fifties, dressed in fashionable attire with an apricot scarf, and spoke with a New York accent. "Where's Sadie?" the psychologist asked.

"She's at preschool."

"I was under the impression I was going to meet her."

"Gee, I'm sorry about that. Sadie has a rehearsal for a skit her class has been working on for weeks. I'll try to bring her next time."

Hudson followed the psychologist into her office and sat in one of the two black leather chairs in front of her desk. He was prepared for the transformation. The lady behind the desk became an interrogator, employing traditional tactics of emotional control and self-confidence. But Hudson skillfully derailed her strategy to build rapport. He adroitly deflected every attempt to extract a statement that Marilyn's parents had the resources and experience to raise Sadie if Marilyn should succumb to cancer. Unable to pry a comment satisfying her primary goal, the psychologist sought an affirmation that grandparents are vital to a grandchild's development. But Hudson addressed both lines of inquiry with a simple and closed-ended response. He said a single devoted dad was a better alternative than relatives two generations removed.

The interrogator was unrelenting. She attacked Hudson from every angle. Hudson's game plan had two objectives: Provide no material that could be used as ammunition, and do not allow her to reach a definitive conclusion about who he was and what his motives were. Some responses gave her the impression he was too dense to understand her questions. Others created the impression he was cunning beyond her expectations.

Hudson was certain that his father-in-law was eavesdropping electronically. Hudson's disgust for this paid shrew intensified when he noticed two anatomically correct children's dolls tucked into the corner of a bookshelf. Those identical dolls had been used to influence the testimony of children in a horrendous sexual abuse case that had generated national headlines. Only after the trial and the convictions did the truth slowly emerge: The children never had been abused. The daycare operator and her staff had been wrongly convicted, publicly vilified, and trapped within a state prison.

The final phase of this thirty-minute mind game circled back to Marilyn: "What exactly are you doing to help your wife battle her cancer?"

"Well, ma'am, I helped her get through her first surgery and I'll help her through the next one. I took care of her after all ten rounds of chemo, and after every round she retched for three days. Sometimes, if she couldn't get to the bathroom, I held the bucket so she could upchuck. I helped her with her colostomy, her meds, her bath, and her home health schedule. I've been running the household, paying the bills, doing the laundry, the shopping, and the cleaning while holding a full-time job. I've been taking care of Sadie twenty-four hours a day, directly or by proxy. When I'm at a work, a nanny looks after her. We all need something to live for, so I try to lift Marilyn's spirits every day. I tell her she needs to be strong for Sadie, because Sadie has to be Marilyn's purpose."

"Of course Sadie is her priority. But what about her other interests?"

"Marilyn loves the beach. After her first surgery I took her and Sadie to a boardwalk and fishing pier. Marilyn was in a wheelchair, and Sadie sat on her lap."

"Was that your only family outing?"

"No. When Marilyn was up to it, all three of us went for drives, usually near the ocean. When Marilyn was in remission, we took a trip out west. Being a Florida girl, Marilyn had never seen a mountain, so I took her and Sadie to Colorado to see the Rockies. That was our last outing." And with that, the session concluded.

* * *

On the day of Marilyn's second surgery, Hudson's alarm detonated at three in the morning. He guzzled coffee, loaded the washer, ironed Sadie's daycare outfit, prepared her lunch, and completed his budget reports. At seven he escorted Sadie into the master bedroom. "Good morning, Mommy!"

"Sadie! Come give me a hug." Sadie climbed into her mom's bed and snuggled. Her mom explained that she and daddy had a busy day, and she'd be home as soon as possible. "You know," Marilyn said, "no matter what happens, I love you with all my heart."

"I love you, Mommy."

At eight, Hudson walked Sadie into daycare. He then returned home and drove Marilyn to the hospital. After a two-hour wait, Marilyn was wheeled into surgery. As always, Hudson waited alone. At four in the afternoon a nurse reported that Marilyn was in recovery and that the surgical oncologist would call Hudson at his first opportunity.

One hour later, Hudson was ushered into the recovery wing, but Marilyn was too groggy to speak. Hudson phoned Marilyn's parents with an update and then picked Sadie up at daycare. He took Sadie to the grocery story, bought her a frozen yogurt at the ice cream shop, and then he drove her to the hospital parking lot. Hudson pointed to Marilyn's window. "When will Mommy come home, Dad?"

"In a few days, I hope. She is very sick. Only God knows when she's coming home."

Sadie turned to her dad and asked, "Will you still be here?"

"I'll always be here for you, sweetheart."

After dinner and a bath, Sadie defeated Hudson at ring toss. He then read her two storybooks before bedtime and, as always, he made up a funny story before saying goodnight.

"I love you, Dad."

"I love you, sweetheart. Sleep well."

Hudson answered the three a.m. call on the half ring. The floor nurse spoke with urgency. Hudson dialed his brother. Four minutes and twenty seconds after he hung up, his brother arrived. Eleven minutes later, Hudson entered Marilyn's room. The scene is forever seared into his gut. His wife, Sadie's mom, was gone.

Agony was carved into Marilyn's once beautiful face. Her death mask was inscribed with pain. The oncologist gently placed his hand on Hudson's shoulder and said, "I'm so sorry. We did everything we could. Her suffering is over. She's with God now."

Despite his pain and anguish, Hudson maintained his equilibrium. His primary concern, preserving his family, now shared a position of equal gravity: "How do I tell a four-year-old that her mother is gone?"

At seven a.m., three hours after signing Marilyn's death certificate, Hudson notified her parents by phone. Marilyn's father took the call. "I'll call you back," he said, whimpering into the phone. Fifteen minutes later, Marilyn's father returned the call: "I think Sadie's grandmother should tell her that Marilyn passed away. I don't mind you telling her, but Sadie's grandmother has to be present. Sadie needs to know that her grandmother will be her new mother."

"Sadie's grandmother is not going to be her new mother. I'm going to tell Sadie, and I'm going to continue to be both her mom and her dad."

"That's ridiculous! You can't do that. You're not equipped. And don't you think for a minute you're going to foreclose on us. We're taking over. I have legal recourse, and I'll use it if I have to, and you'll regret it."

Hudson almost slipped, but he regained his composure and refused to react to the threat. His only response was, "I'll call you later."

Sadie jumped out of bed and nearly collided with her dad in the foyer. They both laughed. Hudson lowered himself, rested his weight upon his knees, and gently placed his hands on Sadie's shoulders. His eyes were moist as he whispered, "Sadie, I have to tell you something. This is the worst news I could ever tell you. I'm so sorry, but I need you to be strong and brave." Sadie started to cry.

"Is this about Mommy?" Sadie asked through her tears.

Hudson dried her tears and wiped her nose with his white cotton T-shirt. "Yes, it's about Mommy." Sadie nodded. Hudson choked and swallowed a sob before saying, "Mommy has been very sick." Hudson paused, centered himself, and said, "I'm so sorry, Sadie." After another pause he asked, "Are you ready?" He flicked the tears running down his face.

"Yes," Sadie said, her eyes and mouth drooping with sadness.

"Mommy passed away last night." Sadie grabbed her dad and clung tight. She buried her face into his shirt as they embraced. Hudson stood in the foyer with Sadie in his arms as they both wept. Finally, Hudson gently lowered Sadie, dabbed his eyes with his T-shirt, and crouched on one knee. He held Sadie close.

"We don't have Mommy anymore," she whimpered.

"We don't, but we have each other."

Hudson stood and executed a maneuver he had developed when Sadie was a toddler. He slid his right arm under his Sadie and hoisted her into his arms. Sadie completed the maneuver by wrapping her arms around her dad's neck. Hudson carried his young daughter into the living room where they sat on the couch near a box of tissues. He dried her eyes and wiped her nose again.

"I never said goodbye to Mommy," Sadie sniveled.

"She knows you love her, and Mommy will always love you."

"But I can't see her."

"You'll be able to feel her. Her love will always be around you," Hudson softly said. "When you say your prayers, keep saying them for Mommy."

"Mommy will hear?"

"Yes."

"She'll hear in heaven?"

"Yes."

"If Mommy is in heaven, can I send a message to her?"

"Well, let's think this through. Where is heaven?"

Sadie pointed to the ceiling and said, "Up in the sky."

"Exactly. So how should we get your message to Mommy?"

"By balloons! We'll send the note to heaven with balloons. It will float to heaven!" Sadie's slightly higher tone conveyed an element of hope.

Hudson responded with a soft and slower pace, perpetuating this glimmer of optimism: "Perfect. Absolutely brilliant idea. What should we do next?"

"I'll write the note and then we'll get balloons."

Sadie tucked her note into an envelope and affixed an adhesive bandage to secure the flap. "Good idea," her dad said. "It's a long flight to heaven."

They bought thirty helium-filled balloons from two grocery stores and secured the note to a dangling piece of the twine they used to connect all the balloons. There was barely enough space in Hudson's SUV for both them and the balloons. The balloons exerted no challenge to the SUV's load-bearing capacity. The weight of the sadness was palpable. Hudson weaved his right arm through the cluster of balloons behind the front seats and grabbed the tip of Sadie's sneaker to reassure her. In the rearview mirror, Hudson observed Sadie push the inflated capsules aside until she had a line-of-sight. When she saw her dad's reflection, she smiled.

Hudson had to leave the rear window partially secured. Had he closed it completely the balloons might have popped. They agreed to launch the helium airship and the precious note from an open field just beyond their subdivision. As they pulled onto the street next to the field, the twine securing the rear window to the latch mechanism snapped, and the balloons escaped. A movie director could not have planned a better moment for comic relief. Sadie giggled, and Hudson ceased searching for the right words to alleviate the pain and the sadness. They quickly parked and watched the balloons ascend to heaven.

Sadie turned to Hudson and said, "Dad, I love you."

"I love you too, sweetheart."

Back in the SUV they watched the balloons fade from view. "Sadie, I have an idea, but only if you're interested. I've been talking to a cat adoption center. Do you think we should get a cat?"

"Can I pick it out?"

"Of course. Do you want a boy or a girl?"

"I want a cat that likes me."

* * *

Hudson fulfilled Marilyn's instructions for her memorial ceremony and cremation. They had agreed that Sadie was too young to be exposed to public displays of grief and sorrow, so Sadie and Hudson would mourn privately. A trusted family friend cared for Sadie during the service. Hudson was the first speaker, and his tear-laced opening set the tone: "We all know life is not fair. Marilyn got cheated. We all got cheated."

After the ceremony and before Hudson picked Sadie up from her caregiver, Hudson fulfilled another request. Marilyn wanted all of her clothing, footwear, and accessories donated to a perinatal hospice center. One hour before the driver was to arrive, Hudson began boxing up the contents of Marilyn's walk-in closet. The draped clothing, alive with Marilyn's scent, brought him to his knees. He recovered in time to meet the driver.

The following morning, Hudson informed Marilyn's parents that he was taking Sadie to the Orlando theme parks for five days. The grandparents invited themselves. Hudson explained that the trip was intended to be a father-daughter healing excursion. Hudson strategically failed to mention the first two days would be spent in Tennessee.

The prospect of raising Sadie in East Tennessee appealed to Hudson. He and Sadie boarded a plane bound for Knoxville later that afternoon. After they were buckled in, Hudson showed Sadie the job pamphlet he had stowed and explained that they might be moving to Tennessee. "What about my cat?" Sadie asked.

"She's part of our family. She's coming with us." They landed in Knoxville just before dinner. The following morning, they met the management team and toured the portfolio of properties. After lunch Sadie played with the children and grandchildren while Hudson met with the directors. The senior executive asked Hudson why he wanted to relocate to Tennessee. "I want to raise Sadie in a wholesome community where there's an emphasis on family," Hudson said. "I don't want Sadie to be pressured by her peers to grow up too fast. Besides, we have to leave Florida."

"Why?"

"Sadie's grandparents are going to make a move to get custody of my daughter. I need to get her out of Florida."

"Hudson, you've been an asset to the company, and your application to relocate has been approved. But I'm a grandmother, and what you're suggesting about Sadie's grandparents I find hard to believe."

After the interview, father and daughter drove to Oak Ridge and walked their future lodging, a two-bedroom apartment on the second floor of a two-story building. The following morning, they checked out of their hotel and drove their rental car to the Knoxville airport for their flight to Orlando.

The day after they returned home, Hudson called the family law attorney recommended by the retired judge. Hudson had absorbed Marilyn's exorbitant medical expenses that were not covered by insurance. Although his capital was shrinking, he agreed to the tall rate of $500 an hour and a $2,000 retainer. Hudson faxed the attorney the executed representation letter. In a separate fax he sent the attorney a copy of the unexecuted custody document that Marilyn's father had pressured her to sign. Upon receiving that second document, the attorney asked his legal assistant to get Hudson on the phone. "How did you get this custody agreement?" the attorney asked.

"The morphine nurse overheard the conversation. She was appalled that they were planning to steal my daughter. The nurse told me where they hid it. I made a copy and put the original back." Hudson briefed the attorney about their recent trip to Tennessee and Orlando and asked him to research the psychologist Sadie's grandparents had required him to meet. "Please check her out. We can't have enough intel."

"This is a unique case, Hudson. Your secret expedition to Tennessee indicates you have a strategy."

"I've distilled this down to the basics. A solid strategy is based on deal points that will not change. I'm relying on two fixed positions: Sadie loves her only parent, and her only parent loves her. I'm also employing a fundamental chess strategy: Control the center, keep the primary character safe and secure, and sacrifice the periphery."

The lawyer called Hudson again the next day: "Your former father-in-law is shopping around for an attorney to handle a custody suit. He tried to set up an interview with me. We never returned his call. He might try to disqualify me as your attorney, but that argument won't fly. They're saying you're unfit to be Sadie's father and that she's at risk. They want the court to intervene immediately and have her evaluated by a therapist of their choosing. You need to understand what you're up against. A child's hearsay is admissible as evidence. If they get five seconds with your daughter, you're finished as her dad. Let me repeat that with emphasis—five seconds and you're finished! They'll claim she said you're hurting her. You and I know what's in your daughter's best interests—to be raised by you, her dad. But armed with manufactured hearsay they'll claim was uttered by your daughter they'll convince the court to remove her and give them custody. This is about what's in their best interests.

"I also checked on that psychologist. She's an absolute demon. She's a skilled hypnotist. She'll hypnotize Sadie into saying what they want her to say, that you've been hurting her, and she's afraid of you. Family law can be a vile business, especially when the custody of a young child is at stake. They don't care that they're destroying your kid's life. As soon as they file here in Florida, you'll be served, and you won't be able to leave the state. If you were to leave after being served, they'd have you arrested on a warrant.

"If you plan on moving to Tennessee, get out of town right now! Establish residency in Tennessee as soon as possible. Liquidate everything that would allow them to claim you have Florida residency, including your house. I'll handle the court appearances and filings here in Florida. Leave now! Call me when you're in Tennessee."

One hour later Hudson and his daughter were packed and motoring north to Tennessee. Their cargo included Sadie's gray tabby, a cat carrier, a litter box, Sadie's stuffed monkey, clothes for one week, toiletries, and Hudson's work files. They crossed the Georgia line at eight that evening and checked into a Valdosta hotel next to an amusement park. Hudson asked the hotel's desk clerk how many Andrew Jackson's were required to circumvent the no-pet policy. Hudson placed a twenty under the signed credit card voucher and agreed to use the back stairwell to transport Sadie's gray tabby. The feline bolted from the room when the pizza delivery arrived. Sadie, Hudson, and the delivery lady ran down the hall after the kitten. Sadie could not contain her laughter. After securing the tabby, enjoying a pizza diner, and watching TV with her dad, Sadie fell asleep on the king bed with her tabby. Hudson stretched out on the couch.

In the morning, the amusement park administrator allowed Sadie's cat to sleep in his air conditioned office while Sadie and her dad enjoyed the park. Sadie loved the thrill of the children's roller coaster, they rode it seven times.

While father and daughter had been driving north to Tennessee, Hudson's younger brother had supervised a team that cleared out Hudson's Florida home. Hudson donated all the furniture, clothing, small appliances, and personal property—including his art and book collections—to charity. He sold the house to his next-door neighbor for the balance on the mortgage. The selling price was $90,000 below market value. "It's just money," he told his brother.

Hudson and Sadie settled into their Oak Ridge apartment. Sadie assimilated into a highly rated private school near their apartment, and Hudson began plying his craft in Knoxville. One week after establishing Tennessee residency, Hudson's Florida attorney called with an update: "Your former in-laws have your Tennessee address. They hired a detective after they discovered you changed the locks and put your house under contract. This morning, they filed a lawsuit in Palm Beach County. I don't want to alarm you, but a processing agent will be serving you in Knoxville. The court is aware that I'm your attorney of record. Your former in-laws are asking for an emergency ruling. They want you ordered back to Florida. The basis of their argument is that Florida is your legal residence, and the case should be heard in Florida. They're also claiming that moving Sadie away from her home in Florida puts her at risk and is an example of your unsound parental judgment. Once you were back in Florida, your days as Sadie's dad would be over. They'll keep filing until they get visitation, and then they'll claim she told them you're hurting her. Then they'll get a court order to have Sadie evaluated by that psychologist. Being ordered back to Florida is tantamount to giving them custody."

"What should I do?"

"I believe I can get most of this first filing thrown out. You relocated to Tennessee for employment, and you did not need their approval or permission to do so. If we do get this dismissed, they'll file another lawsuit within a few days under a different legal premise. They won't stop until they have your kid, and they've got the money to keep this going. You better recognize that they can win."

"I can't let that happen. What if we left the US and went to Israel? Under the Law of Return, we could apply for Israeli citizenship. Do you know about extradition?"

"I do not," the attorney said. "I suggest you check with an immigration lawyer. In the meantime, I'm moving for dismissal. Their attorney is a lightweight, and I can punch holes in his argument. But you need to get yourself a Tennessee lawyer. That shoe is going to drop."

The following morning, an immigration lawyer confirmed that Israel would be a safe haven but given the rapid pace of the expected legal filings and Hudson's financial health, the decision to emigrate to Israel and apply for citizenship would have to be made in short order. With his savings shrinking and legal fees mounting, preserving his capital for a possible move to Israel became paramount. That afternoon, Hudson took Sadie to a local drug store for a passport photo and then to the post office. Upon submitting the passport application, Hudson was told it would take six to ten weeks to process Sadie's passport.

After dinner, Sadie and Hudson discussed school, her new friends, and a planned weekend hike to see the changing leaves. When Sadie was asleep, Hudson headed for the recliner in the living room. He heard a reassuring sound reverberating through the rear casement window. He opened the door to the screened terrace and relished the piercing, high-pitched clicking of the cicadas. Sadie's gray tabby joined him, captivated by the penetrating hum. Returning to the living room to review two commercial leases, Hudson heard the beeping of his answering machine. The illuminated dial indicated seven messages, all from his former father-in-law. All seven held a hostile, menacing tone. After clearing the messages, Hudson answered a live call.

"You better bring her back for your own good. You need to bring her back home to us right now. You took her away from us, and you had no right. I guarantee you the courts are going to award us custody. And if you don't comply, you'll be arrested. What are you doing to her up there in the woods? What horrible things are you doing to her?"

Hudson was certain the call was being recorded, and a reformatted version would likely be introduced as evidence. He responded accordingly: "Do not call me again. Anything you have to say to me you can say to my attorney."

"Oh, what a big man! The big man has an attorney. You have no idea what's coming. We're going to . . ." Hudson hung up. He weighed the merits of moving to Israel instead of fighting this out in the courts, exhausting his capital, and left with no recourse if a judge should award custody to Sadie's grandparents.

Hudson turned the table lamp off and sat on the recliner. A solitary streetlight shining through the front picture window provided a soft, meager glow. In those final conscious moments when thoughts survive the absence of light and illuminate with insight, Hudson envisioned a bridge to a safe harbor. He roused himself from slumber's doorstep and wrote his impressions onto a yellow legal pad: "They may have unlimited funds, but I'm Sadie's dad, and I'm her only parent. How does that not derail their train? Their argument is a violation of natural order and is intrinsically wrong on moral grounds. When natural order becomes subverted by unnatural events, chaos will ensue. I need to protect Sadie from the chaos. There has to be a simple counter position that is so fundamental it eviscerates their legal maneuvers."

After Marilyn crossed over, Hudson vowed that Sadie's appearance would never reveal that she had no mother. As a young man, Hudson knew three female classmates who had lost their mothers. Their heartbreak was evident, and even their wardrobe and their grooming reflected the loss of a mother's touch. It was clear to young Hudson that their fathers did not know how to perform what was then defined as mother's work. It was imperative to Hudson that Sadie always appeared well-dressed and well-groomed. While Hudson practiced austerity with his own budget, he placed no limit on Sadie's. Her wardrobe was crisp and updated with the seasons. Sadie's eye for fashion developed quickly, and so did Hudson's ironing and laundry skills.

Hudson also solved the challenge of sending Sadie to school with a drab and unappetizing lunch. A frozen juice box converted her insulated lunch tote into a refrigerator. The juice box defrosted by lunch time.

Hudson conferred with a cross section of Tennessee contacts and created a list of five child psychologists. He interviewed all five and favored the practitioner with a gentle demeanor and a wall of honors and credentials. "Sadie endured a terrible loss," Hudson explained to her. "I need you to evaluate Sadie's mental health and her grief. Once she knows and trusts you, she might tell you something she wouldn't tell me. I also might need you to testify as an expert witness, if it comes to that."

"Initially, I'll need to see her weekly," the psychologist said while perusing her appointment book. "I have a Saturday slot that will work for all three of us. I'll need a few sessions to gauge the emotional and social trauma of losing her mother. Let's also set up a regular call. Are you available at four every Wednesday afternoon?"

"Yes," Hudson replied. After discussing the fee structure, Hudson and the psychologist set Sadie's first appointment for the following Saturday.

* * *

On the day his case was to be heard by a Palm Beach County judge, Hudson's anxiety spiked. He could think of nothing else. He had contemplated the life of a fugitive, a dad living underground with his four-year-old daughter and her cat. If that was to be his destiny, he would need less than an hour to secure Sadie and her tabby and head out. Their packed bags were just inside the apartment door, and he had stashed enough cash to hold them until he could figure out his next move.

Hudson had no appetite for lunch. Finally, his attorney called at two p.m. and said, "Hudson, I have good news. The case was dismissed with prejudice. The ruling implies that Tennessee is your legal residence. But don't think for a second that you're out of the woods. This is just the first chapter in a Dostoevsky novel. They've hired a bulldog firm with offices in Miami, Tampa, and West Palm, and they're going to file a fresh lawsuit using their rights under the grandparent visitation laws. And case law is leaning in their direction. We won today, but there's an enormous and expensive battle ahead. Any updates on Israel?"

"I applied for Sadie's passport. I hate the thought of leaving the US, but if that's the only way I can preserve my family and protect my daughter, I might have no other option. I better start learning Hebrew. Thank you for handling this. This was the best outcome we could have hoped for."

"Yes, it was. There's something else I want you to know, and I've never done this in twenty-five years of legal counsel. I'm cutting your fees in half. You cannot ask me why."

The following morning, Hudson appealed to a University of Tennessee law school dean for guidance. An older gentleman with a deep affection for Kentucky bourbon, the dean agreed to meet Hudson for cocktails after work. With Sadie under the safe supervision of a loyal female colleague, Hudson arrived by taxi. The hostess directed Hudson to a private corner table.

As the evening wore on, Hudson was convinced this impeccably dressed, articulate fellow was the embodiment of a William Faulkner character. "Mr. Hudson, I need to ask you something," the dean said. "If the roles had been reversed, if you were the one diagnosed with terminal cancer, would your wife had taken care of you the way you took care of her?"

"I've wondered about that, sir. But considering she wanted a divorce and the influence from her parents, I believe I would not have been able to rely upon her."

"Thank you. I do believe I have assessed this conflict. You are seeking liberation for yourself and your daughter, and I admire that. I do want to help you. And please do not be offended, but I have informed the tavern owner that this evening's libation shall appear on my account."

"Thank you, sir. This is greatly appreciated."

"My pleasure." While sipping whiskey, the Southern gent dictated the names of fifteen family lawyers.

That evening, Hudson evaluated the list and identified three finalists. The following morning, he made three appointments. All three lawyers were equally knowledgeable of the law, and all three suggested a similar legal strategy. He retained the lawyer with a piercing glare, an intimidating persona, and autographed photos of football linebacker Jack Lambert and race car driver Dale Earnhardt on his bookcase.

Later that week Hudson called his Florida lawyer. The legal assistant informed him that her boss was in court. The assistant expressed her admiration for his courage and resolve. "If anything ever happened to me," she said, "I'd want my husband to be the kind of dad you are."

"We're not born courageous. We have to learn how to be brave. That's the only way I can get Sadie through this. Although I do everything I can to shield her, Sadie can sense what's going on. Every battle for freedom requires courage, and now Sadie is learning to be brave too." After a slight pause, Hudson shifted gears. "I have to ask you something, and please don't let your boss know that I asked. He told me he's cutting my fees in half. Do you know why?"

"I do, but don't ever tell him I told you. At the hearing, your former father-in-law offered him triple fees and a blank check as a bonus to drop you and take his case. I've been his legal assistant almost five years, and I've never seen him so livid. He didn't file an official complaint, but he told the clerk about it. I'll ask him to call you when he gets back from court."

That afternoon the attorney returned the call: "I got your message to call you back. What can I do for you?"

"There's a fundamental issue that's gnawing at me. In spite of these grandparent visitation laws, don't I have a constitutional right to raise my child as I see fit? Enforcing these grandparent laws will literally destroy the American family. Grandparents would have more rights than parents. This legal concept is upside down. The grandparent visitation laws relegate parents to an inferior position. None of this makes any sense."

"Interesting take," his attorney replied. "It might be a long and drawn out endeavor, most constitutional arguments usually are, and during the process you would have to keep fighting to keep them away from your daughter. This could cost you at least a hundred thousand in legal fees. But your theory might hold water. If you want my research team to look into this they will, but it'll be expensive, and I can't adjust those fees. Do you want me to engage them?" Although Hudson's capital was evaporating, he never blinked.

"Yes. I cannot overlook any angle that could protect my kid. It's worth a shot, even if we're throwing a Hail Mary pass."

"Okay, we're on it. And be advised your former-in-laws will be filing their second Florida lawsuit any day."

On Friday, Hudson received notice from his attorney that Sadie's grandparents had, indeed, filed a second lawsuit.

His former in-laws were demanding immediate, court-authorized access to Sadie under the grandparent visitation laws.

Hudson was able to shelter Sadie from his torment. After Sadie's Saturday session with the psychologist, they hiked a short and mostly level trail in the Great Smoky Mountains. On Sunday morning Sadie attended the youth program at the local synagogue, and in the afternoon she frolicked with friends at a creekside picnic.

On Monday and Tuesday Hudson interviewed the remaining twelve attorneys on the list. Hudson had disqualified fifteen of the most respected East Tennessee family law firms from representing his former in-laws. He believed only second-tier firms could clear the conflict of interest threshold.

On Friday afternoon, Hudson returned to his office to find an urgent message to call his Florida attorney. He prepared for the worst—an emergency legal maneuver granting his former in-laws visitation, a court order to return to Florida, or a judgment to have Sadie evaluated by a court-appointed psychologist. He dialed his attorney from his desk phone: "Hudson," the attorney said, "I need you to sit down."

Hudson exhaled and braced himself. Without Sadie's passport he could not board a flight to Israel. He checked his watch. He would need a minimum of one hour to drive to Sadie's school in Oak Ridge, dash up the street to their apartment to collect Sadie's tabby, their packed bags, and his roll of cash, and make for the Kentucky border. In four hours they could be in a Lexington hotel until he could nuance two seats and a cat carrier on a flight to Tel Aviv. "I'm sitting."

"You're not going to believe this, but your hunch was on the money. There are eight lawsuits in the US challenging the legality of the grandparent visitation laws. All eight are seeking to strike them down as unconstitutional. Every case is similar to yours—upon the death of a spouse, the surviving parent is being sued by the decedent's parents for custody of a minor child. One case has made its way to the Supreme Court."

"When will they hear that case?"

"It's going to take time. Their calendar is loaded. A case like this might take a year or two or even three before it lands on their docket."

"Even if the Supreme Court goes the wrong way, this buys me time. I should have Sadie's passport soon and her cat's vaccine record is up to date. Do you have a gut feeling for how the court will rule?"

"No. We won't know until they publish their opinion. Legal experts are saying it will be a five-to-four vote either way."

"Should we file an amicus brief?"

"You've done your research. Most of my clients wouldn't know about an amicus brief. But we don't need to file. An amicus brief has already been filed, and it's an expensive proposition. I'm drafting a motion to dismiss, subject to the Supreme Court's decision. That motion will freeze them here in Florida. But that won't prevent them from forum shopping and suing you in Tennessee. When they do file in Tennessee, you'll be the only grandparent visitation defendant in the US sued in two states."

"That's a distinction I'd rather not have. Considering the message I was expecting, this is a huge relief. I need to get you paid. When will I receive an invoice?"

"Your first invoice is being mailed this afternoon, and it will include the research team."

"Do you know the amount?"

"Thirteen thousand seven hundred dollars."

"I can't thank you enough. I'll remit as soon as I receive the invoice." Hudson had established a $20,000 budget for all legal fees. He revised his accounting model. He had been crushed by Marilyn's medical expenses, and now his legal fees would exhaust what was left.

Six days later, on a wet Thursday afternoon, the mail carrier delivered the lawyer's invoice to Hudson's Knoxville office. Hudson worked late on Friday evening. Sadie was attending an after school theatrical party. The school administrator told him to pick her up at seven. At six, Hudson was locking the main office door when his desk phone rang. He deactivated the security system, dashed back to his office, and answered the phone.

A North Carolina furniture dealer introduced himself and explained his predicament: "During lunch my banker told me about a program for a low-interest business loan, but to qualify we need a location in another state. Here's my dilemma: The loan program expires on Monday, so the lease has to be executed and notarized by midnight Monday. And I need a big space, at least 15,000 square feet with a loading dock. I've been calling real estate companies in Tennessee for three hours, but I can't reach anyone. Do you have anything?"

"I've got the perfect spot," Hudson said, "and I can move at the speed of light."

Before Sadie's Saturday session with the child psychologist, Hudson and Sadie met the furniture store owner and his management team at the vacant space. Sadie was complemented on how well she operated the flashlights. The lease was executed and notarized on Monday morning just after eleven. After lunch, Hudson submitted his compensation voucher. The result of the calculation was staggering. He recalculated his commission but arrived at the same number. He asked a property accountant to check his math. She confirmed the veracity of the calculation. The box wherein Hudson entered his commission bore the amount of thirteen thousand seven hundred dollars. In the box set aside for additional comments, Hudson wrote, "Divine intervention."

* * *

After dinner on Tuesday, Hudson and Sadie were looking at photos of Pueblo cliff dwellings for a school project. A firm knock on their apartment door shattered the moment. Hudson tensed up. They had no escape options. "You stay here, kiddo. Please stay right where you are and don't make a sound. I'll take care of this," he said as he rose from the dining table. Sadie softly giggled as her tabby leaped off the table and followed Hudson to the door. Hudson peered through the peep hole and observed a middle-aged man in a suit and tie peering back. Hudson recognized the face from a newspaper article about a Baptist church acquiring an adjacent parcel for expansion. "What can I do for you, sir?" Hudson asked through the closed door.

"Please open the door. I'm the senior pastor at the Baptist church, and I'd like to talk to you and your daughter."

"Who sent you, pastor?"

"I just want to help you and your daughter. If you cooperate, any legal action brought against you for kidnapping might be reduced. I decided to visit you before I went to the police. I can set up a meeting with your deceased wife's parents and arrange for your daughter to be returned to them without any further questions. Please let me in. I want to make sure your daughter is okay."

"Pastor, you may mean well, but you've been deceived. Whatever they told you is not true. You're aiding and abetting people who want to destroy my daughter and me. Your actions are inappropriate for a pastor. Do you have children?"

"Yes, a son and a daughter. Why?"

"If, God forbid, your wife should die and her parents sued you for custody of your children, how would you respond to their vicious lies and deceptions? How would you treat people who were carrying out their sick and twisted plans?" The pastor took a step back from the door. His expression changed, his eyebrows scrunched, and his mouth opened.

Hudson's tone softened as he continued: "I can give you my attorney's number, but if you call him, you're going to increase my legal fees. So if you're willing to foot that invoice for his time, please call him. I cannot allow you into our apartment. You came here as an agent for those who would steal my daughter. And you've allowed them to control you emotionally. For all I know, you could provide false testimony that could hurt my daughter in court." Hudson soon heard the pastor descend the metal staircase.

* * *

While driving Sadie to school on Wednesday morning, Hudson spotted two men with binoculars and cameras performing surveillance from the parking lot of the neighboring apartment building. Hudson drove into the lot and opened his window: "This is private property. I work for the landlord, and you're trespassing. If you don't leave right now, I'll call the police. Get out of here, and don't come back!" Hudson quickly jotted down the license plate number.

"We just want to talk to you. We're private detectives. We just want to talk."

"You guys are real pros. I made you in thirty seconds. After I call the police and our attorney, I'm calling the Guinness people. You just set a world record for incompetence." Hudson dialed the police on his mobile phone and said, "I'm reporting two trespassers on private property who are refusing to leave. I want them arrested." The detectives jumped into their van and drove off. Hudson cancelled the call.

Sadie was bursting with laughter as she said, "Dad, you did great."

On Thursday, Hudson retrieved an urgent voice mail to call the local chief of police. The chief wasted little time with introductions: "This morning I received a call from your deceased wife's parents. They're claiming that you kidnapped their granddaughter from them and you're hiding her in my jurisdiction. They also claimed you're hurting her. They asked me to pick her up, detain you, and hold her until they get here. They said they bought a house in North Carolina, and they're only three hours away. I immediately called the city attorney to determine how to proceed. Right after I hung up, I took a call from the FBI field office in Knoxville. An undercover FBI agent in Miami alerted the Knoxville FBI field office of a possible abduction. Your former in-laws are planning to abduct your daughter. They're trying to hire someone to drive a rented car to the Tennessee state line. The Knoxville agent said the grandparents' plan is to grab your daughter and ride with her in the back seat of the rental car. Then they would drive her in their car across the state line to their house in North Carolina."

Hudson was trembling with the adrenaline spike racing through his veins. "Oh, my God! I've got to get to Sadie right now."

"No, you don't. I have a man stationed at her school. She's safe. The school administration is a little upset. I had to inform them."

"I still need to get there. I have to see her. I have a lot of security in place, and I'll reinforce it. But there are times when she's vulnerable. What would you do if you were in my place?"

"The FBI has an abducted child recovery program, but that's only after an abduction. Go see this FBI agent in Knoxville. Have him fingerprint your daughter and get her into the system. And be vigilant."

"Sir, you have no idea how vigilant I am. I barely sleep."

Hudson notified his Tennessee attorney about the pastor's unannounced visit, the encounter with the detectives, and the conversation with the chief. "Follow the chief's advice and meet with the FBI," the attorney advised. "You also need to beef up security around your apartment. Add a security system and more locks. These people are desperate and dangerous. They could pay someone to plant drugs or pornography in your apartment. I'll make some calls and find out which detective firm they used. I've engaged every detective firm from Knoxville to Nashville. Once I find out who those guys were, I'll tell them to cool it, but they won't stop. They live for their fees. You must assume you're always being followed and are under constant surveillance. If you go out to eat, don't even drink one beer in public."

Sadie's classmates began to peel off. Three concerned mothers met with the school principal to discuss seeking

Sadie's resignation from the program. The Sikh family who lived in the apartment below became a reliable ally. Their daughter and Sadie had grown close. The dad, a turban-clad nuclear physicist, told Hudson that in Punjab an attempt by grandparents to steal a child from a rightful parent would be settled in the woods with a knife, and there would be no inquiry. "Fatherhood is sacred," he said.

On Friday afternoon, Hudson picked Sadie up at first dismissal and drove her to the Knoxville FBI field office. A female agent escorted Sadie into the lunchroom for hot chocolate while Hudson reviewed FBI procedures for reporting and recovering an abducted child. Sadie's fingerprints were entered into a national children's database. Hudson provided their histories and handed the agent a copy of Marilyn's death certificate. His status as widower on the identity form repulsed him. As an adolescent he had imagined the possibility of becoming a husband, a father and, perhaps, even a grandfather. The title of widower had been unthinkable.

After dinner, Hudson updated his Tennessee attorney by phone: "You have only one option," the attorney advised.

"Prevent the abduction. If Sadie is abducted, she will be irreparably damaged, and you'll never get her back, even though they would have orchestrated the abduction. I spoke with your Florida attorney, and he agrees with me. Your former in-laws are aware that all they need is five seconds with Sadie, even if those five seconds are the result of an abduction. If they should abduct her we would file an emergency injunction for her return. They would get a court order placing her into a foster home until further hearings could sort it out. And then they'd work the system until they got custody. They would separate the legal fight pertaining to the abduction from the legal battle over custody. They'd pay the driver in cash, and they'd claim they don't know who he is or how to reach him. They'd hire a battery of Tennessee and North Carolina attorneys to handle both cases. That explains why they bought a house in North Carolina, just over the Tennessee line. And by the way, I'm hearing they're making generous campaign contributions."

"So they're willing to terrorize Sadie and put her through an abduction," Hudson said, "and then allow her to be placed into a foster home with a bunch of strangers, away from her dad? This has escalated beyond the legal system, so I can't disclose everything that's running through my mind. I have to keep reminding myself that my concern for Sadie's health and welfare is my firewall."

"Keep it to yourself," the attorney advised. "I don't want to know."

A trusted ally connected Hudson with a licensed firearms dealer, and Hudson purchased a handgun, ammunition, and a gun safe. He also signed up for training sessions at a local firing range. Hudson tightened security procedures with Sadie's school and with the synagogue. He asked the police chief to add the school and their apartment building to the patrol car schedule. A few school and community families also rallied around Sadie and Hudson. Two school dads spoke with Hudson one morning during drop off: "We know you and Sadie are under siege," one said. "They're gonna have to get through us first." Hudson expressed his eternal gratitude. The Oak Ridge office of the management company also stepped up. It was clear that they, too, were willing to put it on the line to protect Sadie.

On the morning of his birthday, Hudson discovered Sadie's hand-drawn card leaning against the coffee maker. At breakfast Sadie suggested a carry-out dinner from the Chinese restaurant so they could celebrate her dad's birthday at home with her gray tabby. Hudson dropped Sadie at school and waved to the patrol car driving through the school lot. Three hours later Hudson received a birthday gift at work, a lawsuit filed in Anderson County, Tennessee. The Tennessee petition demanded immediate visitation under the grandparent visitation laws. The language was nearly identical to the language in the Florida filing. Hudson's Tennessee attorney indicated neither he nor his colleagues knew the opposing counsel. Depositions were set for November, the day before Thanksgiving break.

Hudson's attorney set up two coaching sessions prior to the depositions. Hudson was advised to take only his keys, his Tennessee driver's license, a pen, and a blank writing pad into the deposition room. He was told to leave his wallet and his mobile phone in his SUV. As he was unfamiliar with the process and expecting more treachery, Hudson established a contingency plan. Two hours before the deposition he tucked his passport, Sadie's passport, $10,000 in cash, and the schedules for direct flights to Israel from Dallas, Miami, New York, and Los Angeles into his SUV's spare tire well. He placed a suitcase with two changes of clothes and toiletries into the cargo compartment between a cat carrier and a cardboard box filled with cans of cat food, a bag of cat litter, a new litter box, a plastic bowl, and a cat toy. A lawfully issued Tennessee license plate, gifted to him by an apartment neighbor, a retired Marine, was placed under the front passenger seat alongside a Phillips screwdriver. The fellows in the management company's maintenance department gave Hudson the names and addresses of trustworthy kinfolk living in Kentucky, Arkansas, and Oklahoma. Hudson folded that list into the lockable glove compartment. If the depositions went against him, strengthening the grandparents' case, Hudson was prepared to bolt. His movements would be precise. He would not waste one second. He would collect Sadie and her cat and head for an international airport.

Hudson and his attorney entered the deposition room ten minutes early. Fifteen minutes after the scheduled start,

Hudson's former in-laws and their attorney strolled in. The delay was an obvious maneuver. His former father-in-law placed a briefcase on the conference room table and opened a binder brimming with notes and documents. From the moment they took their seats around the table, the plaintiffs glared at Hudson with hatred and malice. "Let's begin," their attorney announced. "I'm going to start with a series of questions for the defendant."

"No, you're not," Hudson's attorney snarled. "These people are trying to steal my client's child. I'm leading off. For starters, let's get something established right now. Under no conditions will your clients attempt to intimidate my client. They are not to look directly at him. They are not to interrupt my client. If they continue to look at him with that attitude, this deposition is over. Is that understood?" The plaintiffs agreed and immediately focused their gaze upon the conference room table.

Hudson's attorney continued: "Sir, what's in that binder?" he asked Hudson's former father-in-law.

"Those are my personal notes and records. I practiced law in Florida for thirty-three years, and I'm a member of the Florida Bar."

"I want to examine that binder. Please pass it to me."

"I will not," the plaintiff declared. "That's my personal property, and you have no right, sir."

"Under the rules of evidence here in Tennessee, anything brought into a deposition room is subject to scrutiny by counsel. If you do not comply, I have several options at my disposal, including having you arrested." Reluctantly, the binder was passed across the table.

Hudson's attorney proceeded to read aloud the entire contents of the binder, every invoice, every report, every handwritten note and comment, every shred of correspondence, and every unedited, unsubmitted document. He asked the plaintiffs to describe the photos of his client and his daughter that had been snapped by private investigators. Every photo captured an innocent event or interaction between Hudson and Sadie. Keeping the adversary off guard, Hudson's attorney jumped to a fresh topic: He asked the grandparents to confirm that they were holding Marilyn's three-carat engagement ring for Sadie. "We don't have the ring," Sadie's grandfather replied. Sadie's grandmother nodded.

"If you don't have the ring, why do you have this insurance policy identifying a three-carat ring? And the handwritten memo on the policy indicates you remitted payment to renew the coverage."

"Marilyn asked us to renew the policy. As far as we know, your client, the defendant, has the ring," the grandfather said.

After three hours of shredding and debasing the plaintiffs, the deposition broke for lunch. Hudson ate a peanut butter and jelly sandwich in his SUV during the fifty-minute break. After lunch, the annihilation continued. In the second hour after the break, the plaintiffs claimed they had no knowledge of a planned abduction, and they never attempted to hire a driver.

Early in the process, Hudson's attorney had isolated one document. Before addressing that document, the attorney offered a synopsis of the plaintiffs' testimony during the six hours of interrogation: "You apparently hired every private detective firm from Johnson City, Knoxville, Chattanooga, and Nashville, and they produced absolutely nothing. You denied having possession of the three-carat diamond that my client contends his deceased wife asked you to hold in trust for their daughter, Sadie. You denied your attempt to recruit people to participate in an abduction of your granddaughter, a minor child. You denied your plan to drive the abducted minor child across a state line. Do I have to remind you that is a federal crime? You telephoned dozens of influential community leaders including school administrators, city and county commissioners, mayors, police captains, sheriffs, rabbis, and pastors and intentionally misinformed them about my client, your former son-in-law. With absolutely no proof, you defamed and denigrated his reputation. You had the audacity to call his place of employment with those same unsubstantiated, outrageous lies. You were willing to compromise my client's ability to earn a living and support his daughter, your granddaughter. You wantonly misled and misrepresented that my client kidnapped his daughter from you although you never had any form of custody. You ignored the fact that my client is the minor child's biological father and has been the custodial parent and the child's primary caregiver for the child's entire life. You caused irreparable harm to my client and his daughter by insinuating to various third parties that he is harming her. That is what we've learned here today. But I'm not finished. What is this, please?" The attorney slid the document he had set aside across the table.

Hudson's former father-in-law scanned the legal document and said, "That's my sister's certificate of death."

"Please read the cause of death," the attorney instructed.

"It says cancer that metastasized to her breast."

"Please read the entire description so the court reporter has it for the record."

"It says ovarian cancer that metastasized to the breast."

"Why didn't you warn your daughter that she was at risk for ovarian cancer? Don't you think she should have known there was a family history, a predisposition for ovarian cancer?" the attorney asked.

"Because I didn't have the heart to read my sister's death certificate. No one on my side of the family knew," Sadie's grandfather said.

"But you were a practicing attorney, and your sister's death certificate is a legal document. I don't intend to be cruel, but shouldn't you have read it for accuracy, for understanding, and for protecting future generations?" The attorney's question elicited no response.

Upon hearing this testimony, Hudson was in shock and disbelief. His civility suppressed his reptilian rage. Marilyn and her female cousins had been requesting regular mammograms to rule out breast cancer. If only she had known, he thought, Sadie may not have lost her mother.

The questions asked of Hudson during the final hour of the depositions were soft and inconsequential. With his eye on the clock, Hudson's responses were loaded with filler and fluff. Disqualifying the top-rated law firms was a maneuver that was paying dividends. After Hudson, his attorney, and the court reporter vacated the deposition room, the grandparents' attorney asked them about the three-carat stone: "Why didn't you simply explain that you're being good stewards by holding the ring for your granddaughter?"

"Because," Sadie's grandfather answered, "if that bastard gets his hands on that diamond he'll sell it to cover his debts.

We have to keep it hidden. The longer we keep him in court, the deeper in debt he'll be. If we drive him into bankruptcy, he won't be able to hold onto her."

In the parking lot, Hudson asked his attorney for his assessment of the depositions: "They've got nothing," he said, "absolutely nothing. This was a fishing expedition. They were looking for any crack that would allow them to manufacture an argument that Sadie is in danger. I usually stay above the fray, but I don't mind telling you they deserve to go down. But stay watchful. They know they had their butts handed to them today. This was a learning experience for them. Thus far, they've covered their tracks. They weren't going to admit to hiring a driver and planning an abduction. And with no forensic evidence, we can't pin that on them. I wish we could so we could have them arrested. Given their history, they're dangerous. They truly hate you. They want you in a coffin. If they could get away with it, they would pay someone to take you out. They're so blinded by hatred and so filled with their own false superiority they can't recognize that they underestimated you. And they're not going to let you live in peace until they have Sadie and destroy you along the way. But now that we know they have nothing, I'll be asking the court for a dismissal contingent upon the Supreme Court's decision."

* * *

Through the seasons and the birthdays, Hudson remained guarded and watchful. He knew little of peaceful enjoyment. Reports and sightings from dependable sources confirmed that he and Sadie were under surveillance. He was living in the eye of the storm, waiting for the Supreme Court's opinion. If the court upheld the grandparent visitation laws, the backend of the hurricane would be upon them.

Hudson did his best to shield Sadie from his anxiety. Her growth and maturation were sources of wonder. Sadie had enjoyed a stable and happy life in Tennessee for three years, but all of that could implode in a moment.

Hudson's sole priority was to launch Sadie into the world, fully armed, educated, and prepared to make her way. He managed to stay ahead of his legal fees, and he even accelerated his deposits into Sadie's college tuition account.

Although Hudson was planning to travel solo, fate or good fortune intervened. A trustworthy business associate introduced him to a single mom, and they began to date. As the new century rolled in, their relationship crystalized, and they judiciously blended their children into the recipe.

In the depths of an exceptionally cold winter, and just after Sadie's seventh birthday, a synagogue elder arranged for Hudson to meet a retired Israeli security expert who, according to the chatter, had once been associated with Mossad. Hudson and the security expert convened at a luncheonette tucked into the back of a remote convenience store on the Cumberland Plateau. The fellow's suggestions were invaluable. Hudson agreed to never disclose to anyone that they had met and to never reveal the five critical security procedures that had been discussed. Hudson implemented all five measures, and he memorized the directions to three safe houses before destroying the paper napkin on which they had been written.

* * *

On June 5, 2000, Hudson returned to his office and checked his voice mails. In the space of fifty minutes he had received eleven messages. The first voice mail belonged to his Florida attorney: "Call me as soon as you get this message."

Hudson's hands were shaking so fiercely that he misdialed the attorney's number. He calmed himself and redialed: "Great news, Hudson. The Supreme Court struck down a state law that allowed a third party to petition for child visitation rights over parental objections. The Supreme Court just shut your former in-laws down on the grandparent visitation angle." Hudson dried his eyes on his shirtsleeve. "I want you and Sadie to finally live in peace but stay sharp and guarded. They still have other avenues. Remember, all they need is five seconds with Sadie to claim that she told them you're hurting her."

"If the Supreme Court isn't enough to shut them down," Hudson said, "what will it take for us to finally live in peace?"

"Sadie's eighteenth birthday."

Hudson's Tennessee attorney called to congratulate him on the news. He issued similar sage advice: "The grandparent laws were just one way for them to win visitation. A court can still intervene if they can substantiate their claims that Sadie is at risk."

"How do you envision them doing that?" Hudson asked.

"With a witness or with firsthand testimony. Don't rule out your former in-laws paying someone to lie under oath or cooking up another scheme to isolate Sadie. Do not let your guard down. We discussed this in the parking lot after the depositions. You know what they're capable of."

Hudson's supervisor, the senior executive, poked her head into his office and asked, "May I come in?"

"Of course."

"I just heard it on the radio," she said. "I want you to know how happy I am for you and Sadie. Although you never discussed it with anyone in the office, we could feel your torment. I'm proud to have you on our team. When you told me about these people at your interview, I thought you were exaggerating. When I learned they had been calling my staff with stories about you kidnapping your own child, I knew it was even worse than you had described. They're monsters. They were out to destroy you for the crime of being a remarkable father to their granddaughter. I thought I had seen it all, but I never saw anything like this."

Sadie's child psychologist also rejoiced at the news: "I think we can cease our Saturday sessions. You won't need me to testify and, more importantly, there's nothing lurking beyond Sadie's normal and healthy expressions of grief and loss. There are no danger signs. Sadie told me you two speak about her mom and you look through photo albums. That's good therapy. You've been her rock. Every child needs love and security, and that's what you've provided for Sadie through the loss of her mother and the hostilities from her grandparents. Sadie's reliance on you got her through. She's an amazing seven-year-old."

"Thank you. I did for Sadie what she did for me. She got me through. But both lawyers are warning me that it might not be over."

In late September, Hudson received a message to call the police chief. The chief picked up on the first ring. "Hudson, I didn't want to leave for lunch until we spoke. About ten this morning my patrol officer spotted your former in-laws in their gold Mercedes driving through your apartment parking lot. He believes they also drove through the school lot. I alerted the school and asked the patrol cop to stay in the vicinity."

Hudson broke a land speed record driving from Knoxville to Sadie's school in Oak Ridge. A dad greeted him in the parking lot and said, "They may be floating around, but I'm a walking stop sign."

All week Hudson could sense the grandparents' presence. At midnight on Thursday, an automobile flashed his living room window with high-beam headlights. He received hang-up calls at two and four a.m. He had virtually no sleep.

On Saturday morning, Hudson and Sadie began planning the activities for Sadie's eighth birthday party. Hudson observed his former in-laws drive into the apartment parking lot and stop behind his SUV. Hudson recalled a vital piece of advice from the security expert—avoid a confrontation on their terms and conditions. Hudson woke Sadie and told her to get dressed. He alerted his Sikh neighbor by phone and asked him to look after Sadie's cat if they weren't home by dinner. He then called the police dispatcher who agreed to send a patrol car to the parking lot. The gold Mercedes with the Florida plates drove off when the patrol car turned onto the street above the lot. Hudson and Sadie hustled down to the SUV and left for Hudson's office in Knoxville.

Hudson traveled the back roads, his eyes riveted to his rearview mirror. Believing they were not being followed and were out of danger, Hudson parked at the rear of a fast food restaurant. Sadie needed some breakfast. They emerged from the restaurant with a bag of food and a cup of coffee. When they turned the corner, they discovered their SUV was blocked by the grandparents' gold Mercedes. Sadie's grandparents ran toward them. Sadie's grandfather was barking into a mobile phone: "We've got him. We've got the kidnapper blocked in and cornered. Get a police car here immediately!"

Sadie dropped the bag and jumped into Hudson's arms. Hudson tossed his hot coffee onto the grass. Sadie's grandfather closed in and slapped Hudson across the face. Hudson's fedora fell to the sidewalk.

The grandmother tugged on Sadie's feet, pulling her from Hudson's grasp. The grandmother yelled at her husband, "Don't hit him!" Sadie erupted in tears and terror. Hudson rotated his torso, freeing Sadie's shoes from the grandmother's clutch. The grandfather lunged forward, his arm cocked for another strike. Hudson wrapped his arms tighter around his daughter. Hudson slipped his head to the right, and the fisted punch glanced off his left ear.

With Sadie clinging to her dad and screaming with fear, Hudson's only escape route was the busy street. "You bastard!" the grandfather yelled as Hudson ran from the assault. "She belongs to us!"

Hudson began to climb the grass embankment as a police car whisked into the parking lot. The officer quickly surveyed the situation and ordered the grandparents to stand by their car. The officer then motioned for Hudson to return to the lot and took several steps in Hudson's direction, establishing a safe meeting place. Hudson was calming his panic-stricken child, assuring her that no one was going to take her away or hurt them.

A male restaurant patron attired in a postal worker's uniform came forward as an eyewitness. "Everyone in the restaurant saw them attack that man and his kid," the witness said. "I'd be happy to testify. Make sure you get my contact information." During the mail carrier's description of the event, Sadie's grandfather yelled that the witness was Hudson's friend and had been paid to lie. The officer asked Hudson to stay put while he collected the vitals from the grandparents and told them they had no authority to block Hudson's vehicle. He ordered them to vacate. The restaurant manager handed Sadie a replacement meal and a handful of napkins. The officer retrieved Hudson's hat and handed it to him. He then chaperoned Hudson and Sadie to their SUV. The officer and Hudson spoke when they were beyond Sadie's range.

"If you need a witness, you have one. His name, address, and phone number are on the police report. He said he saw them attack you and your daughter. Do you have an attorney? You should get that old guy on assault and battery." When Hudson explained their history, the officer shook his head and rolled his eyes. The officer then handed Hudson the police report and asked if he could escort Hudson and Sadie home. Hudson thanked the officer and declined the escort.

An hour after the attack, Hudson called his attorney to inform him of the incident. At nine on Monday morning a judge read the police report and heard Hudson's testimony. At one that afternoon, Hudson faxed the executed injunction to Sadie's school, the police chief, the FBI field agent, the mayor, several commissioners, the rabbi, his Florida attorney, and various friends and business associates. The injunction prohibited the grandparents from coming about Hudson and Sadie or contacting them in any manner.

* * *

On a chilly winter Sunday afternoon, Hudson hosted Sadie's eighth birthday party at a popular indoor amusement center. Sadie invited her entire second grade class, all fourteen children. Given the security issues, an abundance of dads ushered the partygoers. With Hudson's girlfriend running the function, Hudson kept Sadie in his sights. "I don't blame you," one dad noted. "Must be hard for you to relax."

"You have no idea," Hudson replied. "I haven't had a restful sleep in eight years. We just want a normal life without this extraordinary pressure."

After the party, Sadie attended a sleepover with three of the girls. The host mom had assured the parents that the girls would be in bed at a reasonable hour and that they would be on time for school on Monday.

On Monday morning, Hudson awoke at five. With Sadie out of the apartment he had an opportunity to deep clean her bedroom. Something nudged Hudson to peer out of his second-story living room window. The gold Mercedes with Florida plates was slowly rolling into the parking lot. Only its parking lights were illuminated. The sedan began to back into the loading zone, a section of the lot next to the building and beyond Hudson's view. Hudson contemplated their motives: Were they seeking another confrontation? What if they're setting a trap and paid someone to drive their car? The injunction wasn't issued against the vehicle, and I can't tell who's in the car. If I do call the cops, I'll get roped in. The responding officer would have to interview me, maybe in their presence. I don't want another scene. Hudson called his downstairs neighbor.

The Sikh gentleman and his family dog left their apartment by the back door. They walked through the upper section of the brown grass field behind the building before cutting across the frosty turf and stepping onto the sidewalk. Then they meandered up the gentle hill, stopping at a few trees along the way. While his pooch sniffed a hydrant at the entrance to the parking lot, the Sikh gent subtly removed his digital camera from his pocket. As his dog led him to the cluster of winterberry holly bushes next to the loading zone, he snapped photos of the car's occupants. He captured the license plate when the sedan sped away. Hudson heard his Sikh friend roar with laughter.

With the grandparents having violated the injunction, Hudson's attorney appeared in court with photos bearing the time and date. In chambers, the judge executed an arrest warrant. The attorney then arranged for the warrant to be entered into a database and circulated among neighboring state and local law enforcement agencies. "If your former in-laws take one step onto Tennessee soil, they run the risk of being arrested," the attorney explained to Hudson.

"I think I'll invite them for a barbeque," Hudson quipped.

The attorney notified the Florida Bar Association that an arrest warrant had been issued against a standing member. After performing their normal due diligence and confirming the veracity of the complaint, the matter was forwarded to the judicial referee. Empowered by the referee's recommendation, the Florida Supreme Court permanently disbarred Sadie's grandfather.

On a Saturday afternoon in June, the pastor who had abruptly knocked on Hudson's door called him at his apartment: "I've been thinking about you and your daughter. This is the perfect time for me to apologize. I allowed those people to deceive me. When I got home that night, something directed me to the Book of Psalms, and there it was: 'One who utters lies cannot dwell in the presence of God.' Please accept my apology."

"It takes backbone for you to apologize, pastor. But there's no need. You were doing what you thought was in a child's best interests. The underlying facts that had been presented to you were dishonest, but your intention was honorable."

"Thank you," the pastor said. "The difficult part for me was living with the knowledge that I could have hurt a family when that family was most vulnerable."

"That's true, but thankfully you didn't create any permanent damage. There are many forces tearing apart the nuclear family, and that includes the grandparent laws that could have destroyed mine."

"Tomorrow is Father's Day, Hudson, and you are an exceptional father."

"Soon after I arrived in Tennessee I was contacted by an older relative. He told me I had transformed, that he never expected me to be a good father. I told him I had not transformed, that I'd always been the person I am now. I explained that his perception of me might have changed, but I had not. He never knew me. He didn't know me when I was young, and he didn't know me as an adult. I then reversed roles. I asked what he would have done in the same situation."

"I couldn't have done what you did," he said. "Very few men could have."

"At that moment, my perception of him as a father changed. A father's strength and determination should have no limits."

* * *

With the Supreme Court's opinion etched into bedrock, the injunction in place, and an arrest order on the books, the natural order had been preserved. Hudson and his daughter finally could enjoy the gift of infinite possibilities.

Sadie's bat mitzvah was held at Knoxville's iconic Sunsphere, a twenty-six-story steel truss structure that had been the symbol of the 1982 World's Fair. The mayor supported the notion that celebratory wine was an essential part of the ritual blessing, so Sadie's party became the first function in the Sunsphere's history to allow adult beverages.

Sadie thrived in both middle and high school, and on summer vacations she traveled with her blended family to thirty national parks. They tossed snowballs in Glacier National Park, got drenched descending the steps to the base of Niagara Falls, watched whales along the coast of Acadia National Park, and hiked a trail on the north rim of the Grand Canyon. They laughed at the seals surfing the waves along the coastline of Olympic National Park and were awed in Yellowstone when a snorting herd of bison strolled around their rental car and took a dip in the South Fork of the Yellowstone River.

Periodically, the Tennessee attorney informed Hudson of a letter or a phone call from Hudson's former in-laws. "They're just a nuisance at this point," the attorney said. "I'm telling you about the letters and phone calls only because I'm obligated." On two occasions, Hudson doubled back on his drive to work and tailed the detectives who had been following him.

In Sadie's junior year of high school, she and her stepmom were followed home by a female private investigator who then phoned the house and introduced herself. "I'm a private investigator and I've been hired by Sadie's grandparents. I would like to come over and check on her. I think you and I can work together. As Sadie's nanny you're in a position to do what's right and what's in her best interest. Would it be okay if I came over and met with her? You could sit in if you want."

"I would be remiss if I did not get your full name and phone number. Do you have a license to be a private investigator?" Sadie's stepmom politely asked.

"I do."

"Can I have that information, please?" The investigator recited her full name, phone number, and Tennessee Department of Commerce license number as Sadie's stepmom jotted the details onto a notepad. Sadie had been attending to her chores, she entered the kitchen and was standing next to her stepmom. "Thank you. Now, I'd like you to listen to me carefully. I'm not Sadie's nanny. I'm her stepmom, and this is not the first time you've followed us home. You have been stalking us and that is a violation of Tennessee Code. Now you're harassing us by phone, and I'm recording this conversation. I'm certain my husband will refer this to our attorney and I suspect our attorney will say we have just cause to ask the Department of Commerce to revoke your license. Don't ever phone us again—and stop following us. How can you call yourself an investigator if you didn't know Hudson and I are married?" Sadie's stepmom then calmly returned the handset to the phone's base.

"Did you really record that call?" Sadie asked.

"No. I just told her that. Maybe she'll leave us alone now." Sadie exploded with laughter.

On Sadie's eighteenth birthday, Hudson's attorney authored a registered letter to Sadie's grandmother that demanded the return of the three-carat stone. The letter went unanswered. Without empirical proof, Hudson had no legal recourse. "They stole your kid's ring," the attorney said. "At least they didn't steal your kid."

"It's just money," Hudson said. "Sadie has her whole life in front of her, and she has an unalienable right to pursue happiness. And that is priceless."

Those who observed Sadie's ascent into adulthood relished the journey. Her achievements were plentiful, the missteps few. Every accomplishment became another steppingstone. Graduating high school with honors, earning a four-year professional degree, and backing that up with a graduate degree were, indeed, flagstones on that path. So too were her real estate moves. She bought a starter home when she was twenty-three and, five years later, traded-up for a larger house on a wooded lot. The mortar on that path was her strength, self-confidence, and independence.

Many believe it is unwise to live in the past, and to a great extent Hudson practiced that notion. He held no regrets and held little interest in turning the calendar pages against the grain. Hudson ceased pondering how a thoughtless law could be twisted into a destructive weapon of terror. How could he and Sadie be punished for a crime he never committed? And yet Hudson never lost sight of where he and Sadie came from or where they landed. He would never forget the toxic assault they had to endure to arrive at that landing. The poison strengthened their core and sharpened their steel. Hudson believed there had been something else at play, a power beyond his perceptions. Hudson discovered he had an answer to every question his mind could conjure. On certain rare and solemn occasions he sensed a connection to the unseen, a connection to a vitality that runs through every living thing. Beyond those esoteric nudges he was, and always shall be, connected by flesh and blood to his daughter.

About the Author

Sheltering in a log cabin in East Tennessee with an English wife, two orange tabbies, and a spent collection of Scotch whisky bottles, this dad, real estate broker, tennis fan, and comedy historian is edging ever closer to the formula for powdered whisky.

www.ingramcontent.com/pod-product-compliance
Lightning Source LLC
Chambersburg PA
CBHW060507300726

48975CB00008B/2686